This book belongs to

Written by Rosie Greening.
Illustrated by Lara Ede.

Don't you dare brush my hair!

Lara Ede • Rosie Greening

make
believe
ideas

This is **Clare**.

She loves her **hair**.

Take a **look**
(but please don't **stare**).

Claire's daring with her **hair** each day.

she doesn't **care** what people say.

She decorates
her swirly **locks**
with **snacks** and **cats**
and pairs of **socks**.

Here's the thing **Clare** doesn't do.
(This sounds **SHOCKING**, but it's true.)
No matter what gets **stuck** in there,
Clare will never

BRUSH HER HAIR!

But every time the **brush** comes out,
Clare stands firm and starts to shout…

The snack-packed **hair** soon starts to **smell**,
and **flies** begin to buzz as well.

Her friends all wince and **disappear**,
but still **Clare shouts** for all to hear...

"Don't you dare brush my hair!

It's meant to look like this, I swear!
Why are you **obsessed** with germs?
Hair is **better** stuffed with **worms!**"

But without a **brush** or trim,
all that **smelly** stuff stays in.

And as each **season** comes and goes,
the stinky **hair** just **grows** . . .

SUMMER

SPRING

FALL

WINTER

...and **grows.**

At last, all **Clare** can see is **hair**:
it's absolutely everywhere!
She cannot **see** or **hear** or **walk**,
and soon poor **Clare**
can't even **talk!**

FON'T FOO
FARE
FRUSH
FY FAIR!

IS **ANYONE**
THERE?

Mom says, "I can use SHAMPOO!"

Dad says, "I have **brushes** too!"

Clare's friends bring **styling stuff** galore:

this is what they've waited for!

They **brush** it,

trim it,

wash it lots,

untie the **tangles**

and the **knots**.

"I feel like a **brand-new** me! I can **move** and I can **see**.

I think my **messy** days are **gone**. I'll always **brush** it from now on."

Everyone sighs with **relief**. **Clare** is still there underneath! The **hair** looks **GREAT** for **one** whole day,

until it's time . . .

... for **Clare** to **play!**